The Nutcracker and the Mouse King

Ernst Theodor Amadeus Hoffmann

Adapted by Schmuel Chocron F.

CHAPTER 1

Christmas Eve

On Christmas Eve, the children of Doctor Stahlbaum were not allowed into the family room, let alone the adjoining living room.

Evening had come, and Fritz and Marie Stahlbaum sat huddled in a corner. As was usual on Christmas Eve, no-one had brought in a light, and so they sat in an eerie darkness.

Fritz was whispering to his younger sister Marie (who had just turned seven) how early that morning, he had heard rattlings and poundings from the forbidden chambers, and how he had just seen a small, dark man slipping a large box under his arm across the corridor, and how he knew it was none other than Godfather Drosselmeier.

Marie's eyes lit up, and she clapped her hands and cried, "Oh, what do you think Godfather Drosselmeier has made for us?"

Now, Judge Drosselmeier was not the least bit handsome. He was small and thin with a face full of wrinkles, and where his right eye ought to have been he wore a black eyepatch. He had no hair at all on his head, and so he wore a cleverly-made white wig of glass threads. In general, Godfather Drosselmeier was a clever sort of man who knew a great deal about watches and clocks and even made some himself. When one of the Stahlbaum family clocks was sick and couldn't sing, Godfather Drosselmeier would come and take off his glass wig and yellow coat and put on a blue apron. He would then stab all sorts of sharp instruments into the clock. Marie felt sympathy pains, but the clocks weren't at all hurt. In fact, the clocks purred and sang as joyfully as ever, which made the whole family happy again.

Drosselmeier always had something in his pockets for the children when he came to visit. Sometimes it was a funny little man who rolled his eyes and bowed, sometimes it was a box from which a small bird hopped, and sometimes it was something else. But every Christmas, the judge would go to extra effort to create something spectacular - so spectacular that the children's parents would put it away for safekeeping afterward.

"What do you think Godfather Drosselmeier has made for us?" Marie anxiously asked.

Fritz said it probably wouldn't be any different this time. He expected a fortress where soldiers marched and drilled about. Other soldiers would come to overtake it, but brave soldiers inside the fortress would fire booming cannons to keep the intruders away.

"No, no," Marie interrupted, "Godfather Drosselmeier told me of a beautiful garden with a big lake, with beautiful swans swimming around wearing gold necklaces and singing pretty songs. Then a little girl comes to the lake and calls the swans, and feeds them marzipan."

"Swans don't eat marzipan," Fritz said scornfully. "And Godfather Drosselmeier can't make a whole garden. Besides, they always take what he gives us away. I prefer what Papa and Mama give us; we can keep those and do what we want with them."

The children continued to guess and wonder. Marie pointed out that her large doll, Madame Trudie, was more awkward than ever these days. She fell on the floor time and again, which put nasty marks on her face and was getting her dress filthy. She'd tried scolding her, but to no avail. Also, there had been the way Mama had smiled when she saw how happy Marie was with the little parasol for Gretchen. Fritz pointed out that his father was quite aware that his stables were missing a chestnut horse and that he was short of an entire cavalry.

The children were certain their parents had bought them many wonderful presents, and that through the blessings of the Christ Child (who looked down upon them with kind, loving eyes), Christmas presents were much better than any other presents. Their older sister Louise added that the Christ Child, who brought them gifts through the hands of their loving parents, knew much better what they would like than they, so rather than wishing and hoping they should remain patient and quiet. This gave Marie pause for thought, but Fritz muttered, "I'd still like a chestnut horse and some hussars."

Night had fallen, and Fritz and Marie huddled together in silence. It suddenly seemed there was a rushing of wings and a distant, but beautiful music. A bright light touched the wall, and the children knew that the Christ Child had flown away on shimmering clouds to other happy children. At that moment, a silvery bell rang and the doors flew open.

"Ah-ah!" The children froze as they stepped on the threshold, but Papa and Mama lead them inside by the hand.

"Come in and see what the Christ Child has brought you."

CHAPTER 2

The Gifts

I ask you, the reader, to remember your most wonderful Christmas. Remember the beautiful, colorful presents and the lavishly decorated Christmas tree? You should be able to imagine how the children felt. With sparkling eyes, the children were completely silenced for awhile. Then Marie gave a deep sigh, and said "Oh, how beautiful... oh, how nice."

Fritz made a few exuberant leaps into the air. They must have been very good that year, because they had never been given so many wonderful and magnificent presents before. The big fir tree in the center of the room was covered in golden apples, silver apples, buds, and blossoms. Besides that, there were sugared almonds, colorful candies, and many other delicacies. Each and every branch was adorned, and best of all, hundreds of lights sparkled from within its branches like tiny stars. Its warm and inviting glow beckoned the children to pluck its fruits.

Around the tree were such colorful and lovely gifts to defy description. Marie saw the prettiest dolls and all sorts of neat little items and tools for them. What especially caught her eye was a dress hanging from a rack so it could be seen from all sides. It was made of silk and adorned with colorful ribbons, and after admiring it for a moment, Marie exclaimed "It's so beautiful! Oh, I love it! Surely I'll be allowed to wear it!"

Fritz had already galloped three or four circles around the tree on his toy horse, which he had found bridled next to the table. After dismounting he said it was a wild beast, but that was all right - he'd tame it sure enough. Then he inspected his new squadron of hussars, who were dressed handsomely in red and gold. They carried tiny silver weapons and rode on horses so white that they almost looked like they were made of pure silver.

When the children quieted down they turned to the picture books, which were filled with beautifully-drawn pictures of flowers, children at play, and colorful people. They were so life-like that one could almost believe they might really move or speak.

They had scarcely begun to delve into the books when the silvery bell rang again, and they knew Drosselmeier's gift was ready. They ran to the table, where a silken screen Drosselmeier had been behind all along was lifted up. Sitting upon the table was a green lawn decorated with flowers, and upon that sat a beautiful miniature palace with many golden towers, delicate little mirrors, and windows to see the elegant rooms inside. A bell rang, and the palace's doors opened. Inside, ladies with long dresses and gentlemen with plumed hats walked about the halls. There were so many candles burning in the silver chandeliers in the central hall that the whole room seemed to be on fire. A gentleman in an emerald cloak would presently poke out of a window, wave, and return into the palace again. Likewise, by the door of the castle, a miniature

Drosselmeier - no bigger than Papa's thumb - came out to wave at the children before returning inside.

Fritz had been watching the whole scene with his hands on his hips. Presently he said, "Godfather Drosselmeier, let me go into the castle!"

The judge gave him a disparaging look, and for good reason. Fritz was quite foolish to even suggest such a thing, for he was far too big to fit inside the tiny castle - its golden towers weren't even as tall as he was.

After watching the lords, ladies, children, the emerald-cloaked man, and the miniature Drosselmeier moving through their routines for awhile, Fritz said impatiently, "Godfather Drosselmeier, come out of the other door."

"That cannot be done, Fritzkin," the judge responded.

"Then let the man in green come out and walk with the others."

"That cannot be done, either."

"Let the children come down. I want to see them up close."

"It cannot be done," the judge said flatly. "Once it has been put together, it cannot be changed."

"So," Fritz said dramatically, "then nothing can be changed? If that's how it is, then all your pretty little people don't mean much to me. I think my hussars are better, because they can go forward or backward on my command, and they're not locked up in any house."

And so Fritz sprang to the Christmas table, where he let out his squadrons mounted on silvery horses to trot, turn, charge, and fire to his heart's content.

Marie had also quietly slipped away, because she too had begun to find the walking and dancing dolls dull. But unlike Fritz, she was too polite to show it.

"A machine like this isn't meant for simple children," the judge said angrily to their parents. "I'm going to pack it up."

But their mother came over and asked to see the inside of the castle and the intricate clockwork that made the dolls move. So the judge took everything apart and put it back together again, which cheered him right up. He gave the children some beautiful brown men and women with gold faces. They smelled as sweet and pleasant as gingerbread, and both Fritz and Marie enjoyed them very much.

At their mother's request, their sister Louise had put on the new dress she had received, and she looked very beautiful in it. But when Marie was asked to wear hers as well, she said she'd rather simply look at it, which she was gladly permitted to do.

CHAPTER 3

The Favorite

Marie had lingered near the Christmas table when the others had left because she had seen something nobody else seemed to have noticed. After Fritz had disengaged his hussars from parading about the tree, a splendid little man became visible. He stood there quietly and modestly, as if waiting his turn.

His build left much to be desired: aside from the fact that his stocky and somewhat long upper body didn't quite fit his small and spindly legs, his head was much too large. However, his fine clothing suggested that he was a man of taste and education: he wore a beautiful hussar's jacket of vivid violet with lots of white trimming and buttons with matching trousers. He wore the most beautiful pair of boots that a student, or even an officer, had ever worn. They were so tight on his legs that they seemed to be painted on.

Somewhat amusingly, a narrow and clumsy cloak was attached to his back that seemed to be made of wood. He also wore what looked like a miner's hat on his head. However, Marie remembered that Drosselmeier wore an awful morning coat and an equally dreadful hat, but nevertheless was a kind and loving godfather.

It also occurred to Marie that if Drosselmeier were to dress as elegantly as the tiny man, he would not look nearly as handsome.

She had quite fallen in love with the tiny man at first sight, and the more she looked at him, the more she could appreciate his good-natured face. His light green eyes, though protruding, were kind and friendly. The craftsman who had given him his combed white beard had done a fine job, for it made his sweet red smile stand out even more.

"Oh!" Marie exclaimed at last. "Papa, who does the charming little man at the tree belong to?"

"That," her father said, "that, dear, will work hard for all of you to crack many a tough nut, and he belongs as much to Louise as to you and Fritz."

He gently removed the little man from the table and lifted up his wooden cloak. His mouth opened wide and wider, revealing two rows of sharp, white teeth. At her father's behest, Marie put a nut into the little man's mouth and - crack! - the nut's shells fell away, and the sweet meat inside fell into her hand.

Her father then explained that the Nutcracker - for that is what the tiny man was - had descended from a long line of Nutcrackers. The children shouted with joy, and Dr. Stahlbaum said, "Marie, since you're so fond of the Nutcracker, you can look after him. But remember, Louise and Fritz have as much right to use him as you."

Marie immediately took the Nutcracker into her arms and gave him nuts to crack, though she always chose the smallest so he wouldn't have to open his mouth very wide, as she felt it wasn't very attractive. Louise came over to use the Nutcracker, and their new friend cracked nuts for her, too. His friendly smile made it seem that he was happy to serve them.

Fritz presently grew tired from his drilling and riding, and when he heard his sisters cracking nuts he went over to investigate. He laughed heartily at the funny-looking little man.

Now Fritz wanted to eat nuts, and the Nutcracker was passed from hand to hand between the three of them. Fritz shoved the biggest and toughest nuts into his mouth. Suddenly, there was a dreadful cracking sound that wasn't from the shell of a nut - and three teeth fell out of the Nutcracker's mouth, and his jaw hung loose and wobbly.

"Oh! My poor dear Nutcracker!" Marie wailed, and took him from Fritz's hands.

"He's a naive, stupid amateur," Fritz declared. "He probably doesn't even understand his own craft. Just give him to me, Marie, and he'll crack nuts for me, even if he loses the rest of his teeth - or even his good-for-nothing jaw."

"No, no!" Marie had begun to cry. "You can't have my dear Nutcracker. Look at how sadly he looks at me and shows me his wounded mouth! You're a cold-hearted person! You've beaten your horses and you even had a soldier shot!"

"It had to be done. You don't understand these things," Fritz said. "The Nutcracker is mine, too, so give him to me."

Marie began to cry harder and wrapped the injured Nutcracker in her little handkerchief. Then their parents came in with Godfather Drosselmeier, who to Marie's dismay took Fritz's side.

However, her father said, "I have specifically placed the Nutcracker into Marie's care, which I can see he clearly needs right now, so no-one may take him from her. Also, I'm very surprised at Fritz - as a good soldier, he should know that an injured man is never sent out to fight."

Fritz looked very ashamed of himself, and without another word concerning nuts and nutcrackers crept off to the other side of the table, where he posted some of his hussars as look-outs and sent the rest to bed for the night.

Marie found Nutcracker's lost teeth and tied a pretty white ribbon from her dress around his injured jaw as a bandage. The poor fellow looked pale and frightened, so she held him more carefully than before, as if he were a small child, and looked at the beautiful pictures in the new picture-books, which were now among the other presents.

Marie became quite angry - which was was quite unlike her - when Godfather Drosselmeier laughed and continually asked how she could humor such an ugly little man so.

The Nutcracker's odd similarity to Drosselmeier came back to Marie's mind, and she said very seriously, "I'm not sure, dear Godfather, if you were dressed like my dear nutcracker and had such nice shiny boots, whether you would look as nice as he does."

Marie had no idea why her parents suddenly laughed so loud, or why Drosselmeier's nose turned so red, or why his laugh seemed so weak. There was probably some reason for it.

CHAPTER 4

Wonders

As you enter the Stahlbaum family living room from the front door, to your left is a beautiful glass-fronted cabinet in which the children keep all of the wonderful things they receive every year. Louise was still very small when their father hired a skilled carpenter to build the cabinet, and he used such brilliant panes of glass and set them so skillfully that anything you put inside looked brighter and prettier than when you held it in your hands.

In the highest shelf (too high for Fritz and Marie to reach) were Godfather Drosselmeier's works of art. On the shelf below were the picture-books, and on the two shelves below that Fritz and Marie could put whatever they wanted, though it always happened that Marie put her dolls on the bottom shelf and Fritz quartered his soldiers on the shelf above it.

And so tonight Fritz put his hussars in the second shelf, and Marie moved Madame Trudie out of the way to make room for her new doll in the beautifully-furnished room and invited herself in for sweets.

As I've said, the room was very beautifully-furnished, and that's the truth. I don't know whether you, my attentive reader, have such a nice miniature flower-print sofa, charming little chairs, an adorable tea-table - and best of all, a bed with a bright and shiny frame for your most beautiful dolls to rest on. Everything stood in the cabinet's corner, where the walls were papered with colorful little pictures, and you can well imagine that the new doll Marie had received (whose name was Madame Clarette, as Marie had learned that evening) was quite content with her quarters.

It was now very late - almost midnight, and Godfather Drosselmeier had long since gone home. But the children did not want to leave the cabinet, so their mother had to remind them that it was time for bed.

"You're right," Fritz said finally. "The poor fellows-" (referring to his hussars) "-want a little peace and quiet, and they don't dare nod off while I'm still around!" And so Fritz scampered off.

But Marie said, "Just a little while longer, just a minute. Leave me here, Mama. I have some things to take care of, and once I finish I'll go straight to bed."

Marie was a trustworthy child, so her mother knew she could leave her alone with the toys without worry. Still, she was concerned that Marie might be so distracted by her new doll and the other new toys that she might forget to put out the lights before leaving, so Mrs. Stahlbaum extinguished all of the lights except for the one that hung from the middle of the ceiling, which cast a gentle, graceful light into the room.

"Come to bed soon, dear, or you won't be able to get up on time!" she called as she left for her bedroom. Once Marie was alone, she hurried to do what had been on her mind, something that she wasn't sure why she hadn't been able to mention to her mother earlier. She carried the injured Nutcracker to the table and gently set him there, where she unwrapped her makeshift bandages to see the wound. The Nutcracker was very pale, but he smiled a kind, sad smile that wrenched her heart.

"Oh, Nutcracker," she said softly, "I know Fritz hurt you badly, but he didn't mean any harm. It's just that his wild soldier's life has made him a little hard-hearted, but otherwise he's a very good boy. I promise I'll take very good care of you until you're healthy and happy and can use your teeth and stand with your shoulders straight. Godfather Drosselmeier will fix you up, he knows all about-"

Marie could not finish what she had started saying because when she had said the name "Drosselmeier," Nutcracker's face had turned up in disgust and his eyes shot green sparks. But just as she became frightened, Nutcracker looked at her with his kind, sad smile again. Marie realized that the awful face she had seen was only a trick of the light caused by the flickering lamp above.

"I'm not a silly girl who gets scared so easily, who thinks that a wooden doll could make faces!" Marie told herself. "But I love Nutcracker because he's so funny and kind, which is why he must be looked after - which is proper."

So Marie took her friend the Nutcracker into her arms and took him to the glass-fronted cabinet, where she knelt down in front of it. "I request, Miss Clarette, that you give up your bed to the injured Nutcracker, and manage with the sofa as well as you can. Remember, you're quite healthy and full of energy, because otherwise you wouldn't have such round red cheeks - and anyway, very few dolls - even the most beautiful - have such a comfortable sofa."

Madame Clarette looked very grand and morose in her Christmas finery, but she didn't make a peep.

"What else can I do..." Marie wondered. She took the bed out of the cabinet and gently laid Nutcracker upon it, still wrapped in a beautiful waist-sash from his sore shoulders to above his nose.

"He can't stay with naughty Clarette," she said, and lifted the bed along with the Nutcracker up to the second shelf, where she placed it next to the picturesque village where Fritz had stationed his hussars. She locked the cabinet and was making her to make her way to her bedroom when - pay attention now! - a quiet whispering and rustling sound came from behind the stove, the chairs, and the walls. The clock whirred over them, but it didn't strike. Marie looked up at the clock, and the large gold-painted owl that sat on the top had lowered its wings so that the whole clock was covered, and its ugly cat-like head and beak jutted forward. What's more, the owl seemed to be speaking with audible words:

Tick-tock, Stahlbaum clocks, only whir and purr
Mouse-king is so sharp of ear (whir whir, purr purr)
Only sing the old song (whir whir, purr purr)
Ding dong, ding dong.

I promise you, he won't last long

Marie was now terrified and was just about to run away when she saw that Godfather Drosselmeier, not the owl, was sitting on top of the clock. What she had taken for wings were really his yellow coat tails.

Marie gathered up what little courage she had left and cried up tearfully, "Godfather Drosselmeier! Godfather Drosselmeier! What are you doing up there? Come down and stop scaring me, you bad Godfather Drosselmeier!"

But suddenly there was a great commotion all around - first a shrill giggling and squeaking, then a pitter-patter like a thousand tiny feet behind the walls, and then a thousand tiny lights peeping out from the cracks in the floorboards. No - not lights! They were small, twinkling eyes! From every crack and crevice, mice had begun to squidge and squeeze their furry gray bodies into the room. Soon there were packs of mice running back and forth everywhere, until they all stood in rank and file just as Fritz would position his soldiers before a battle.

Marie thought they looked quite cute (unlike some children, she was not at all afraid of mice), and her fear had all but passed when a squeal so shrill and sharp pierced the air that it made ice-cold shivers run through her back! And oh, what she saw!

Now dear readers, I know that you're just as clever and courageous as young Commander Fritz Stahlbaum, but I honestly think if you had seen what stood before Marie's eyes, you would have run away, jumped into your bed, and pulled up the covers high above your ears.

But poor Marie couldn't run to the safety of her bedroom, because - listen! - just in front of her feet, a plume of sand, lime, and brick shards spouted into the air as if by some underground force, and seven mouse heads with seven shining crowns rose hissing and squeaking from the ground. Then up came a mouse's body, at whose neck all seven heads were attached. The mouse army gave three cheers in unison upon the arrival of this horrendous beast.

The mouse army had been sitting until now, but now they hopped to their feet and set themselves into motion. They hopped right toward the cabinet - and toward Marie, who stood near it. She was so terrified that her heart beat so violently she thought it might jump out of her chest and she would die. Then her blood seemed to stand completely still in her veins.

Nearly fainting, she stepped backward - and with a crash and a tinkle, shards of glass fell from the cabinet doorpane, which she had accidentally pushed her elbow into. She felt a very sharp pain in her left arm, but her chest untightened and she no longer heard the squeaks and squeals of the mice. Everything had become completely quiet, and although she didn't look she believed that the noise of the breaking glass had frightened them into scampering back into their holes.

But wait! What was that? Just behind Marie, in the cabinet, a small, delicate voice began: "Awake! Awake! Onto battle! This very night! Awake! Awake!"

And then there was a beautiful and musical tinkling of bells. "Oh, that's my miniature carillon!" Marie exclaimed happily. She jumped quickly to the side and looked inside the cabinet. There was a strange glow coming from within, and several dolls were running helter-skelter with their small arms waving about. Suddenly, Nutcracker rose up, threw off his blanket, and jumped with both feet out of the bed, and loudly shouted:

Crack crack crack!
Stupid mousepack!
Squeaking, squealing!
Gnawing, clawing!
Crack crack crack!
Stupid mousepack!

And Nutcracker drew his little sword, brandished it in the air, and shouted, "my dear vassals, friends, and brothers, will you assist me in this difficult fight?"

Three scaramouches, a Pantaloon, four chimney sweeps, two zither players, and a drummer immediately shouted, "Yes, my lord! We will loyally follow you through death, victory, and battle!"

Inspired by the Nutcracker's speech, they made the dangerous leap down from the second shelf to the floor.

They were not at all hurt because, not only were they dressed in soft wool and silk, there wasn't much inside them other than cotton and sawdust. So they plopped down like little sacks of wool.

Nutcracker, on the other hand, would have almost certainly broken himself to pieces. He he two feet to fall to the ground, and his body was as brittle as linden wood. Indeed, he would have likely broken his arms and legs had not Madame Clarette sprang from the sofa and thrust herself out from the bottom shelf to catch the Nutcracker (who had descended brandishing his sword) in her arms.

"Oh, good dear Clarette!" Marie cried. "I've misjudged you so badly. I'm sure you were happy to give the Nutcracker your bed!"

But Madame Clarette spoke now, embracing the young hero in her silken chest. "Please, my lord, as injured and sick as you are, do not go into the battle. See how your courageous vassals are ready to fight and how certain they are of victory. Scaramouche, Pantaloon, chimney sweep, zither player, and drummer are already down, and you can see that the standard bearers on my shelf are moving. Please, my lord, either rest in my arms or watch your victory from the brim of my feathered hat."

Thus Clarette spoke, but Nutcracker refused to be still and kicked his legs until she had no choice to put him down.

Nutcracker politely bowed on one knee and said, "my lady, I will always remember your grace and compassion in combat and strife."

Then Clarette bent down so she could take Nutcracker by the arm. She gently lifted him up, quickly took off her sequined cincher, and tried to put it about his shoulders as a cape. But he took two steps back, put his hand on his breast, and said solemnly, "please do not waste your favors on me, my lady, because..." he paused, then tore off the ribbon that Marie had put about his shoulders and pressed it to his lips. He let it fall, and it hung from him like a field bandage.

Brandishing his sword, he jumped as nimbly as a bird over the ledge of the bottom shelf and down to the floor.

You have probably noticed, observant reader, that the Nutcracker had felt Marie's love and kindness before he was properly alive, which is why he preferred Marie's simple white ribbon over Clarette's, even though it was quite shiny and looked very pretty.

And what now?

As Nutcracker jumped down, the squeaks and squeals began again. What a noise! Under the big Christmas table, the deadly hordes of mice waited, and over all of them the monstrous mouse with seven heads loomed.

What will happen next?

CHAPTER 5

The Battle

"Strike the battle march, loyal vassal drummer!" Nutcracker shouted. The drummer beat his drum so furiously that the glass in the cabinet shook and reverberated the sound. A rattle and clatter came from within the cabinet, and Marie saw that the lids of the boxes where Fritz's army was quartered had popped open. The soldiers were jumping out of their boxes and forming regiments on the bottom shelf.

Nutcracker was running back and forth shouting words to inspire his troops. "I see that dog of a trumpeter isn't moving himself!" he cried furiously. Then he quickly turned to Pantaloon, who had become quite pale and whose long chin trembled. To Pantaloon he said, "General, I know how courageous and experienced you are. We need a quick eye and a quicker mind, so I'm trusting the cavalry and artillery to you. You don't need a horse - your legs are so long you can gallop quite well on them. Now, do your job."

Pantaloon immediately put his long, spindly fingers into his mouth and trumpeted so loud that it may as well have been a hundred trumpets. From within the cabinet, there came a nickering and stamping. Marie looked inside and saw Fritz's dragoons and cuirassiers, and especially his new hussars dropping down to the floor. With flags flying and music playing, regiment after regiment marched marched across the floor and lined themselves up into neat, wide rows.

With clanks and clinks, Fritz's cannons were brought to the front. Boom! Boom! Boom! they went. They fired tiny balls of sugar - no bigger than peas - that exploded and covered the mice in powdered sugar upon impact. Although it didn't really hurt, it was very demoralizing.

Meanwhile, an artillery battery up on Mama's footstool was doing a considerable amount of damage - they were firing volleys of peppernuts, which took down many of the mice.

Yet the mice continued to advance, even overtaking some of the cannons. And there was now so much noise, smoke, and dust that Marie could barely make out what was going on. But one thing she could tell for sure was that both sides were fighting as hard as they could. Sometimes it seemed that the toys would win, and other times it looked like the mice would take the victory.

Yet the numbers of mice were increasing rather than decreasing, and the small silver pills they shot with great skill had already begun to strike the glass-fronted cabinet. Madame Clarette and Madame Trudie anxiously paced inside and wrung their hands.

"Am I to die in the flower of my youth? I, the most beautiful of dolls?" Clarette asked.

"Was I so well-preserved, just to die here in my own home?" Trudie asked.

Then they fell into each other's arms and cried so loudly that they could be heard above the commotion outside.

And what a commotion it was! You can hardly begin to imagine the noise! Cannons boomed and clanked, tiny muskets fired, the Mouse King and his mice squeaked, and the Nutcracker shouted orders from amidst the cannons.

Pantaloon, to his credit, had lead some brilliant cavalry charges, but the mouse artillery had pelted Fritz's hussars with foul-smelling balls that left stains on their red jackets. Because of this, they lost the will to advance.

Pantaloon ordered them to turn left. Caught up in the excitement of giving orders, he himself also turned left - and so did his cuirassiers and dragoons. And so they all marched left and went home.

This left the battery on the footstool unprotected, and it wasn't long before a swarm of very ugly mice came and knocked the whole thing over - stool, guns, and gunners alike.

Nutcracker looked very worried and ordered the right wing to retreat. Those of you who have lead any battles yourself will know that retreating is no different than running away, and I'm quite sure that you feel just as sorry as I do that things turned out so badly for the army of Marie's beloved Nutcracker.

But let us turn from this now and look at the left wing of Nutcracker's army, where everything is still going well and there is hope for the soldiers and their general.

During the worst of the battle, cavalry mice waiting quietly under the bureau threw themselves upon the left wing of the Nutcracker's army with horrible squeaks and squeals - but what resistance they found!

Slowly, because of the difficult terrain (that is, the edge of the cabinet), the standard-bearers under the command of two Chinese emperors had moved over and formed a square. These brave, colorful, and splendid troops consisted of gardeners, Tyroleans, Tunguses, barbars, harlequins, lions, tigers, monkeys, apes, all of whom fought with composure, courage, and determination.

With Spartan bravery, this elite battalion would have snatched the victory from the hands of the enemy had not a bold captain of the mouse cavalry daringly bitten off the head of one of the Chinese emperors, who in turn killed two Tunguses and a monkey as he fell. This formed a gap that the enemy could penetrate, and soon the whole battalion had been gnawed through.

But the enemy gained little advantage from this unfortunate turn of events, because every mouse who viciously bit into the middle of his valiant opponent got a printed piece of paper lodged in his throat and he immediately choked to death.

Despite this small gain, things were looking bad for the Nutcracker's army. Once they had begun to fall back, they found themselves falling back further and further and losing more people until all that remained was a small group backed against the cabinet.

"Bring up the reserves!" Nutcracker ordered. "Pantaloon, Scaramouche, Drummer, where are you?" He was hoping for fresh troops from the glass-fronted cabinet.

Some brown men and women with golden faces, hats, and helmets appeared, but they were so awkward with their swords that they were no help at all. The only thing they managed to knock down was General Nutcracker's hat. The enemy chasseurs had soon bitten off their legs, and when they fell they crushed and killed several more of the Nutcracker's men.

The enemy drew closer still, and there was no escape. Nutcracker would have jumped up to the cabinet's ledge, but his legs were too short. Madame Clarette and Madame Trudie could not help him, for they both laid in a faint. Hussars and dragoons sprang past him into the cabinet. In desperation he called out, "a horse! A horse! My kingdom for a horse!"

But that that moment, two enemy marksmen took hold of Nutcracker's wooden cloak and held him fast. Squeaking in triumph from seven throats, the Mouse King sprang forward to take his kill.

Marie could no longer keep what little composure she had, and without really knowing why she removed her left shoe and threw it as hard as she could into the thickest patch of mice she could see - right at their king. At that moment, everything faded from Marie's vision. She felt a stabbing pain in her arm, and fell fainting to the floor.

CHAPTER 6

The Illness

Marie awoke from a deathlike sleep to find herself in her own bed. The sun was shining through the window, making the frost on the panes sparkle and shimmer.

Sitting nearby was a stranger - no, Dr. Wendelstern, the surgeon. "She's awake now," he said in a soft voice.

Her mother came over and looked at Marie with frightened, searching eyes.

"Oh Mama, dear, are all the mice gone? Is good Nutcracker safe?"

"Don't talk about nonsense like that, Marie. What do mice have to do with the Nutcracker? You've been a very naughty child and worried us very much. That's what happens when a child is willful and doesn't do as her parents tell her. You played with your dolls until you became sleepy, and it may be that a mouse - which I find unlikely - jumped out and frightened you, and you fell back and pushed your arm through the glass. Dr. Wendelstern, who removed the glass from your arm, says if you'd cut an artery you might have been left with a stiff arm - or bled to death. Thank God I woke up after midnight and noticed you weren't in your bed. I went into the living room and found you passed out in front of the toy cabinet, bleeding heavily. I almost fainted from shock myself, and then I saw Fritz's soldiers, a lot of other dolls, and broken banners, gingerbread men, and not far away, your left shoe."

"Oh, Mama, Mama!" Marie interrupted, "don't you see - that's what was left of the battle between the dolls and the mice. The mice wanted to take the Nutcracker and I got scared, so I threw my shoe at them - and after that, I don't know what happened."

Dr. Wendelstern glanced at Mrs. Stahlbaum, then said to Marie very gently: "There's no need to worry, my dear child. The mice are all gone and Nutcracker is safe in the toy cabinet."

Then the physician (that is, Marie's father) came in and spoke with Dr. Wendelstern for a considerable length of time. He took Marie's pulse, and she heard mention of wound fever. She had to stay in bed and take some medicine for a few days, though aside from the pain in her arm she didn't really feel ill or uncomfortable.

She now knew that Nutcracker had escaped the battle safe and sound. Occasionally, she would hear as if in a dream the Nutcracker's voice, distinct yet weak. "Marie, dear lady, I already owe you so much, but there is more you could do for me!"

Marie tried to think of what it could possibly be, but she could think of nothing.

She could not play with her toys because of the pain in her arm, and the illustrations in the picture books swam before her eyes until she had to give up on them. And so time seemed to draw on forever. She could hardly wait for evening, because then her mother would come and read her all sorts of beautiful stories.

One evening, her mother had just finished the story of Prince Fakardin when the door opened and Godfather Drosselmeier stepped into the room. "Now I must see for myself how the sick and injured Marie is doing," he said.

As soon as Marie saw his yellow coat, the image of the Nutcracker losing the battle against the mice came back into her mind. Automatically she said: "Oh, Godfather Drosselmeier, you were so ugly! I saw you up there on the clock, covering it with your wings so it couldn't strike and scare away the mice. I even heard you call the Mouse King! Why didn't you help the Nutcracker or me, you ugly Godfather Drosselmeier? It's your fault that I'm hurt and sick and stuck in bed, isn't it?"

Marie's mother, shocked, asked, "what is wrong with you, Marie?"

However, Godfather Drosselmeier made an odd face and said in a rasping, monotonous voice:

The pendulum had to purr and pick
It could not strike, nor could it tick
But now the bells sound loud and strong
Dong and ding, ding and dong
Doll girl, don't be afraid
The king of mice has gone away
The owl returns now swift and quick
Pick and peck, peck and pick
Bells ring, dong and ding
Clocks whirr, purr and purr
Pendulums must also purr
Clink and clank, whirr and purr

Marie stared wide-eyed at Godfather Drosselmeier. The judge looked somehow uglier than usual, and his right arm was moving back and forth as if he were manipulating a marionette. Marie would have been very frightened had it not been for her mother's presence, and for the fact that Fritz (who had quietly crept in) suddenly burst out in loud laughter.

"Oh, Godfather Drosselmeier, you're too funny today," Fritz said. "You're just like the jumping jack I threw behind the stove awhile back."

But their mother had a serious expression on her face and said, "Dear Mr. Drosselmeier, what odd entertainment. What is it all about?"

"Heavens!" the judge responded with laughter. "Don't you know about my watchmaker's ditty? I always sing it to patients like Marie." He quickly sat close beside Marie's bed and said, "Don't be angry at me for not putting out all fourteen of the Mouse King's eyes, but I've got something for you that I think will make you really happy." With those words, he reached into his pocket and swiftly pulled out the Nutcracker. His missing teeth had all been set firmly back in and his wobbly jaw was set straight again.

Marie shouted with joy, and her mother said, "See how well Godfather Drosselmeier thinks of Nutcracker?"

"You still have to admit, Marie," Drosselmeier interrupted, "he's quite ugly. I'll tell you how such ugliness came into his family, if you want to listen. Or maybe you already know the story of Princess Pirlipat, the witch Mouserinks, and the clockmaker?"

"Wait a minute," Fritz said suddenly, "you've fixed the Nutcracker's teeth and jaw, but he's got no sword - why's he missing a sword?"

"Oh!" Drosselmeier responded indignantly, "you have to complain about everything, boy! Why should I find him a sword? I've fixed his body; it's up to him to get a sword if he wants one."

"That's true," Fritz said. "If he's any good, he'll know where to find his weapons."

The judge turned again to Marie. "So, Marie, do tell me - do you know the story of Princess Pirlipat?"

"Oh, no," Marie said. "Do tell, dear godfather - do tell!"

"I hope, dear Mr. Drosselmeier, that your story won't be as horrible as the ones you usually tell," her mother said.

"Not at all, dear lady," Drosselmeier replied. "On the contrary, the story which I have the honor of telling is a fairytale."

"Tell us the story, dear godfather!" the children begged, and so he began.

CHAPTER 7

Tale of the Hard Nut

Pirlipat's mother was the wife of the king and therefore the queen, and that made Pirlipat a princess from the very moment she was born. The king was beside himself with joy at the sight of his beautiful little daughter. He whooped and hollered and swiveled around on one leg and cried out again and again: "Oh, joyous day! Have you ever seen anything more beautiful than my Pirlipat?" And the ministers, generals, and staff likewise spun on one leg and cried, "No! Never!"

Anyone who had seen the little princess could not deny that she was probably the most beautiful little girl in the whole world. Her face was like the finest lily-white and rose-red silk ever woven, her lively little eyes were like two sparkling azure stones, and her curly hair was like threads of pure gold. In addition, Princess Pirlipat had come into the world with two rows of pearly-white teeth, which she used for the very first time when she bit the finger of the chancellor who tried to get a better look at her face. The chancellor cried out "oh, jiminy!" Or maybe it was "that hurt!" Opinions to this day are divided on the matter.

But Pirlipat had most certainly bitten the chancellor's finger, and the delighted kingdom knew at once that their princess was spirited, sharp, and clever.

All were cheerful and merry - all except the queen, who looked anxious and fearful for reasons no-one knew. In addition to the two guards standing outside the door of the princess's room, the queen had ordered that six female attendants sit closely around her cradle every night. What seemed completely mad and utterly incomprehensible to everyone, however, was that each attendant had to hold a tomcat on her lap and stroke him so that he never stopped purring.

It's impossible for you dear children to guess why Pirlipat's mother gave these orders, but I know, and I shall tell you.

It had happened some time ago in the royal court that many splendid kings and excellent princes were gathered. It was a marvelous affair - there were jousts, comedies, and dancing. In order to show that he wasn't at all lacking in gold or silver, the king took a sizable sum out of the royal treasury to do something really spectacular.

Having heard from the head chef that the court astronomer had privily told him that now was the proper time for slaughtering the livestock, the king ordered the preparation of a lavish sausage feast. Then he threw himself into his carriage and invited all of the kings and princes to have a "spoonful of soup" so he could enjoy their surprise when they saw what he really had planned for them.

Then he approached his queen and said very kindly, "you do know, sweetie, how I like sausages."

The queen knew what he meant - that she, as she had done in times past, should take up the useful job of sausage-making. The chief treasurer immediately had the golden sausage boiler and silver casserole dishes sent to the kitchen, a roaring fire of sandalwood was set ablaze, and the queen put on her damask apron. It wasn't long before the delicious smell of sausage soup wafted out of the boiler and into the council of state.

The king was seized with such delight that he could not contain himself. "Pardon me, gentlemen!" he shouted, and leapt away to the kitchen where he hugged the queen and stirred the soup with his golden scepter. Feeling much better, he returned to the council.

The crucial moment had come in which the fat had to be cut into cubes and roasted on silver grills. The ladies-in-waiting left the kitchen because the queen wished to perform this task alone out of love and devotion to her royal spouse.

As soon as the fat began to sizzle, a tiny little voice called out: "Give me some of that fat, sister! I'm also a queen, and I deserve to feast, too! Give me some fat!"

The queen knew that it was Lady Mouserinks. Lady Mouserinks had lived for years in the palace and claimed to be related to the royal family and even queen of of a realm called Mouseland. She also claimed to have a large court under the stove.

The queen was a good and charitable woman, so although she didn't recognize Mouserinks as a queen or a sister she was willing to let her enjoy the feast as well. "Come out and you may have some of my fat," she said.

Lady Mouserinks jumped out, hopped up to the stove, and grabbed piece after piece of fat from the queen in her delicate little paws. But then came her cousins, aunts, uncles, and her seven sons, and the latter were such unruly brats that they ran all over the fat and the terrified queen could do nothing to stop them. Fortunately, the head lady-in-waiting came in and chased away the unwanted guests before all of the fat could be gobbled up. The court mathematician was called in, and he calculated how best to distribute what was left of the fat among the sausages.

Trumpets and drums sounded. The kings and princes arrived - some on white horses, some in crystal coaches, and all in their best clothes. The king greeted them cordially, then sat down at the end of the table in kingly dignity with his crown on his head and his scepter in his hand.

During the liver sausage course, the king gradually grew paler and he raised his eyes toward the heavens. A sigh escaped his chest, as if some enormous pain was digging at his insides.

During the blood sausage course, he fell back into his chair sobbing and moaning, with both hands over his face. Hearing the king's wailing and howling, everyone jumped up from the table. The court physician tried in vain to take the unfortunate king's pulse. A deep, nameless misery seemed to be tearing him up.

Finally, after much persuasion and attempts to use the strongest remedies available (feather quills and such), the king stammered in a barely audible voice, "too little fat."

The queen threw herself at his feet in despair and cried, "oh, my poor unfortunate royal husband - oh, what pain you've had to endure - you see the guilty one here at your feet. Punish - punish her hard - Lady Mouserinks and her cousins and uncles and aunts and seven sons have eaten the fat..."

With that, the queen fell back in a faint.

The king jumped up and demanded, "Chief lady-in-waiting, how did this happen?"

The chief lady-in-waiting told him all she knew, and the king decided to take revenge on the Lady Mouserinks and her family. The privy council was summoned, and it was decided that Lady Mouserinks would stand trial and all her property would be confiscated. But the king was worried that Lady Mouserinks and her family would go on eating his fat in the meantime, so the task of solving the problem was given over to the clockmaker and wizard.

The clockmaker, whose name is the same as mine - Christian Elias Drosselmeier - promised to rid the palace of Lady Mouserinks and her family forever. He created many small and very intricate little machines into which a piece of fat was placed and set near the home of Lady Mouserinks.

Lady Mouserinks was too clever to fall for it herself, but despite her warnings all of her cousins, aunts, uncles, and even her seven sons went after the fat. Just as their greedy little paws reached for the fat, a grate slammed shut trapping the lot of them. Then they were promptly taken to the kitchen and executed in disgrace.

Fearing for her life, Lady Mouserinks left the castle with what family she had left. Grief, despair, and rage filled her chest.

All of the royal court cheered - all except the queen, who was worried. She knew what sort of woman Lady Mouserinks was, and that she would not let the deaths of her sons and other family members go unavenged. Indeed, Lady Mouserinks appeared one day when the queen was preparing another one of the king's favorite dishes and said, "My family is dead - take care, my queen, that the Mouse Queen does not bite your little princess to pieces! Take care!"

Then Lady Mouserinks disappeared from sight. The queen was so startled that she dropped the food she was preparing into the fire. For the second time Lady Mouserinks had spoiled one of the king's favorite dishes, which made him very angry.

Well, that's enough for tonight - I'll tell the rest later."

As much as Marie, who had her own thoughts about the story, asked her godfather to tell the rest of it, he refused. He jumped up saying, "too much at once is unhealthy. I'll finish it tomorrow."

Just as the judge was about to leave through the door, Fritz asked, "but tell me, Godfather Drosselmeier - is it really true that you invented the mousetrap?"

"How can you ask such a silly question?" their mother asked him.

But the judge smiled strangely and said quietly to Fritz, "am I not a clever enough clockmaker that I could invent a mousetrap?"

CHAPTER 8

Continuation of the Tale of the Hard Nut

"Now you well know," the judge told the children the next evening, "why the queen was keeping their beautiful princess so carefully guarded. How could she help but worry that Lady Mouserinks would return and make good on her threat to bite the princess to death? Drosselmeier's contraptions were of no use against the clever and shrewd Lady Mouserinks, and the court astronomer, who was also the royal family's private astrologer, had said that Mr. Purr and his family would be able to keep Lady Mouserinks away from the cradle. Therefore it happened that every attendant was ordered to hold a tomcat on her lap and stroke his back to make his job a little less tedious.

One night at midnight, one of the attendants woke from a deep sleep. The room was as silent as death; there was not a purr to be heard. One could have heard the woodworms nibbling at the timbers.

Then she saw a large, ugly mouse standing on its hind feet near the princess's face. With a frightened cry that woke everyone else, the attendant jumped to her feet. Lady Mouserinks (for it was none other) ran into a corner. The cats ran after her, but they were too late - she disappeared into a crack in the floor. Just then, Pirlipat woke up from the noise and began crying pitifully.

"Thank Heavens, she's alive!" they said.

But what horror awaited them! Instead of an angelic little face and a perfect little body, a hideous and huge head was attached to a shrunken and shriveled body. Her sparkling little azure eyes had become staring green eyes that almost looked as if they'd pop out of her head, and her sweet little mouth now stretched from ear to ear.

The queen shut herself away in mourning, and the the walls of the king's study had to be padded because he would very often bang his head against the walls and cry most pitifully, "Oh, what an unhappy monarch am I!"

One might think that he might have realized that it may have been better to go on eating his sausages without fat and leave Lady Mouserinks and her family in peace under the stove, but he didn't. Instead, he put all the blame on the court clockmaker and wizard, Christian Elias Drosselmeier of Nuremberg, and issued him an order: restore the princess to her former self within four weeks or find a cure that was certain to work, or suffer the disgraceful death of beheading.

Drosselmeier was in no small state of terror, but he trusted in his craft and in luck and set to the first thing that seemed useful to him. He carefully took the little princess apart without harming her and examined her internal structure, but all he could discover was that the larger the princess grew, the worse her condition would become.

He put the princess back together again and sat down by her cradle in despair, which he was not allowed to leave.

It was into the fourth week - Wednesday, in fact - when the king looked at Drosselmeier with eyes flashing in rage and cried, "Christian Elias Drosselmeier, cure the princess - or die!"

Drosselmeier began to cry bitterly, but Princess Pirlipat happily cracked nuts. For the first time, Drosselmeier took note of the princess's unusual appetite for nuts, which she cracked with the very teeth she had been born with. In fact, the princess had cried for hours after her transformation until a nut chanced to roll by. She promptly snatched it up, cracked it open, ate the core, and immediately quieted down. Since then, all attendants were advised to bring nuts whenever they came in.

"Oh, holy and unfathomable instinct of nature, present in all things!" Christian Elias Drosselmeier cried, "you now show me the door to the answer to this mystery; I will knock, and it will open!"

He immediately requested to speak with the court astronomer, and was lead by guards to him. Both men tearfully embraced each other, for they were close friends. Then they went together into a secret room where they consulted many books concerning instincts, sympathies, antipathies, and other such mysteries.

When night fell, the astronomer looked to the stars, and with the help of Drosselmeier (who was also quite familiar with astrology) took the princess's horoscope. It was no easy task, for the lines of the stars were so crossed and tangled. But at last, it became clear that in order to break the curse and restore the princess's beauty, all she would have to do is eat the sweet core of the nut Crackatook.

Now, the nut Crackatook had such a hard shell that you could run the wheel of a cannon over it without breaking it. This nut had to be given to a young man who had neither yet shaven nor worn boots, and he would have to bite it open before the princess and give the core to her with his eyes closed. What's more, he could not open his eyes until he had taken seven steps backward without tripping or stumbling.

Drosselmeier and the astronomer worked for three days and three nights. That Saturday, the king had sat down for his midday meal when Drosselmeier (who was scheduled to be executed the following Sunday) joyously rushed into the room and announced that he had found the means to restore the princess's lost beauty. The king gave Drosselmeier a fierce bear hug and promised him a diamond sword, four medals, and two new Sunday suits.

"After lunch, I expect you'll get to work on this," the king added amiably. "And I trust, excellent wizard, that you'll make sure that this young man with the nut Crackatook in hand hasn't had any wine to drink so he doesn't trip when he goes walking seven steps backward like a crab. Afterward, he can drink all he wants."

Drosselmeier was dismayed at this and with trembling and fear informed the king that they neither begun to search for the nut or the boy to crack it, and it was uncertain whether nut or nutcracker would ever be found.

The king waved his scepter high above his head in a rage and roared, "then the beheading shall proceed as scheduled!"

Fortunately for Drosselmeier, the food had tasted particularly good that day and the king was in a better mood than usual. This made him more open when the queen, who was touched by Drosselmeier's distress, and asked that he reconsider. Drosselmeier gathered his courage and explained that he had indeed found out how to cure the princess, and had therefore rightfully won his life back. The king decided that Drosselmeier was stalling with silly excuses, but after taking a tonic for his stomach he announced that both the clockmaker and astronomer should set off on foot and not return until they had the nut Crackatook in their possession. The queen suggested that they could find the man to do the cracking by regularly placing advertisements in local and foreign newspapers.

And here the judge broke off again, and promised to tell the rest of the story the next evening.

CHAPTER 9

The End of The Tale of The Hard Nut

On the third evening, the lights had barely been lit in the Stahlbaum house when the judge returned to finish his story:

Drosselmeier and the astronomer searched for fifteen years without coming across the nut Crackatook. I could spent four weeks telling you children all about the places they went and the strange things they saw, but I'll just say that Drosselmeier, in his deep sorrow and disappointment, began to feel a longing for his beloved home city of Nuremberg. A particularly nasty attack hit him when he was smoking his pipe with his friend the astronomer in the middle of some great forest in Asia. And suddenly he cried:

"Oh, beautiful beautiful Nuremberg, my beautiful hometown Nuremberg, whom I have not seen for so long, though I've traveled to London, Paris, and Petrovaradin, they cannot fill my heart and I must always ask of you. Oh, beautiful city of Nuremberg, with your lovely houses and their windows!"

Drosselmeier's cries were so sorrowful that the astronomer felt deep compassion for him, and he began to cry and wail as well. In fact, his cries were so loud that they could be heard through a sizable portion of Asia.

Then he wiped his eyes and said, "Esteemed colleague, instead of sitting here pining away over Nuremberg, why don't we go to Nuremberg? After all, it doesn't matter where we search for that accursed nut."

"True," Drosselmeier said. He brightened up a little. They both knocked the ashes out of their pipes and straightaway headed from the middle of Asia to Nuremberg. No sooner than they had arrived, Drosselmeier went to see his cousin, the dollmaker, painter, and gilder Christoph Zecharias Drosselmeier, whom he had not seen in many years. The clockmaker told him all about Princess Pirlipat, the Lady Mouserinks, and the nut Crackatook. The dollmaker clapped his hands in amazement and said, "what a marvelous story!"

Drosselmeier further related his adventures, of how he had spent two years with the King of Dates, how the Prince of Almonds had disdainfully rejected him, how his search at the Society of Natural Science in Squirrelton had yielded nothing, and how he had failed everywhere to find even a trace of the nut Crackatook.

Through the story, Christoff Zecharias frequently snapped his fingers and turned around on one foot. Finally he exclaimed, "well, that'd be the devil, wouldn't it!" and threw his hat and wig into the air. He gave the clockmaker a hug and said, "Cousin - cousin, all your troubles are over because unless all the world has conspired to deceive me, I own the nut Crackatook!"

He immediately brought out a box from which a pulled a gilded nut of moderate size. "Behold," he said. "Many years ago, a nut seller with a bag of nuts came into town around Christmastime. He got into a fight with a local nut seller who didn't think he had any right selling nuts here right outside my shop and had to set his bag down. Then a heavily-loaded cart drove over it and broke all of the nuts except one. The stranger offered it to me, with the oddest smile, for a twenty from 1720. Strangely enough, that's just the coin I found when I checked my pocket. So I bought it and gilded it without really knowing why I paid so much for it or why I'd wanted it so badly."

Any doubt that the nut wasn't really Crackatook was soon lifted when the astronomer scraped off the gold gilding and found the word "Crackatook" engraved in Chinese characters. The joy of the travelers was immense and his cousin was the happiest man under the sun when Drosselmeier told him that his fortune was made, for he would soon receive a handsome pension and plenty of gold for gilding.

Both wizard and astronomer had just put on their nightcaps and were ready to go to bed when the latter said, "My esteemed colleague, good fortune never comes but in packs - not only have we found the nut Crackatook, but also the young man to break it and present the princess with the core of beauty! No, I cannot sleep now," he said excitedly, "I must draw up this young man's horoscope this very night!" With that, he tore off his nightcap and began at once to observe the stars.

Christoph Zechariah's son was a handsome boy who had never shaved and had never worn boots. In his early childhood he had been a jumping-jack for a few Christmases, but there was no trace of that now as his father had taught him how to be a proper gentleman. During the Christmas season (which was now) he wore a red coat trimmed in gold, a sword, a hat carried under his arm, and an excellent wig. Thus he stood splendidly in his father's shop and gallantly cracked nuts for young girls - and for this reason they had nicknamed him "Nutcracker."

The next morning the astronomer gave the wizard a hug and said, "here he is! We have him! Now, there are two things we must not ignore. First, you must make your splendid nephew a sturdy wooden tail that attaches under the jawbone so that his jaw can be firmly shut therewith, and then we must not reveal that we have the young man who will crack the nut when we arrive at the palace, but instead he must wait for some time to reveal himself for I have read in the horoscope that after a few young men have broken their teeth on Crackatook, the king will promise the kingdom and the hand of the princess in marriage to whoever can crack the nut open and restore the princess's beauty."

The dollmaker was pleased to have his son marry the princess and become prince and later king, so he gave him up to the travelers. The little wooden tail Drosselmeier attached to his hopeful young nephew's head worked so well that he was able to crack the hardest of peach pits.

Drosselmeier and the astronomer reported to the palace that they had found the nut Crackatook, and the palace immediately issued requests for young men who might break the nut. Many arrived to try their own sturdy teeth on the nut and restore the princess, including a few princes.

Our two travelers were considerably startled when they saw the princess. Her shriveled body with its tiny hands and feet could hardly carry her enormous head. The ugliness of her face was enhanced by a cotton-white beard that had sprouted around her mouth and on her chin.

Everything happened exactly as the astronomer predicted: young men with shoes on their feet and peach fuzz on their faces bit down on the nut Crackatook and only got a few broken teeth and a sore jaw for their troubles without helping the princess in the slightest. Every young man who had injured himself thus would be carried away half-fainting by specially-appointed dentists. Many could be heard sighing, "that was a hard nut!"

The king, now fearing that his daughter might never be restored, promised the kingdom and the princess to whomever could crack the nut. At that moment young Drosselmeier stepped out and asked if he could try to crack the nut.

None of the other young men had caught the princess's eye the way young Drosselmeier had. She put her little hands over her heart and sighed, "oh, let it be this one who breaks the nut and becomes my husband!"

After paying his respects to the king, queen, and princess (the latter especially politely), he took the nut from the Grand Master of Ceremonies. He put it in his mouth and tugged at the tail Drosselmeier had made for him, and - crack crack! - the shell broke into many pieces.

The young man removed the fibers from the core of the nut, closed his eyes, gave it to the princess, and began his seven steps backward. The princess swallowed the core and - oh, wonders! - an angelically beautiful young lady stood before them with a face of lily white and rose red, eyes like azure, and hair like curled strands of gold. Trumpets and drums mingled with the cheers of the people. The king and his court danced on one leg as they had the day of the princess's birth, and the queen had to be revived with strong-smelling perfumes because she had fainted from happiness.

The commotion did not at all ruffle young Drosselmeier, who was just taking his seventh and last step. But then who should pop out of a crack in the floor but Lady Mouserinks, ugly, squeaking, and squealing - and right under the young man's heel. This caused him to stumble so that he almost fell. Oh, calamity! The boy was instantly as hideous as Princess Pirlipat had been a few moments ago. His shriveled body could hardly hold up his ugly head with its protruding green eyes and hideously wide smile. Instead of the little tail the clockmaker had made for him, a small wooden cloak hung from his shoulders that controlled his jaw. The clockmaker and astronomer were beside themselves with horror.

Then they saw Lady Mouserinks roll onto the floor. Her malice had not gone unavenged, for the pointed heel of young Drosselmeier's shoe had hit her sharply and fatally in the neck. The fear of death had seized her, for she squeaked and squealed piteously:

"Oh, Crackatook, hard nut, now I must die
Hee hee, pee pee
Nutcracker, young man, you too will die

My seven-crowned son will avenge my death
And take from you your living breath
Oh life, so vibrant and red, I - squeak!

With that, the mouse queen died and was promptly carried to the royal furnace for disposal.

In the heat of the moment everyone had forgotten the young Drosselmeier, but the princess reminded the king of his promise and he immediately ordered that the young man be brought before them. But upon seeing how hideous the unfortunate boy had become, the princess held her hands over her face and cried, "take him away! Take that horrible nutcracker away!"

The chamberlain seized him by the shoulders and threw him out the door. The king was furious that someone had tried to give him a nutcracker for a son-in-law and blamed everything on the clockmaker and astronomer, whom he banished forever. None of these developments had been in the horoscope taken at Nuremberg, but the astronomer was not deterred from reading the stars again, which now revealed that young Drosselmeier would become a prince and a king despite his ugliness. Furthermore, he could lift the curse put upon him if he could defeat the seven-headed mouse born to Lady Mouserinks after the death her seven sons and find a lady who would love him despite his looks. You may have seen young Drosselmeier in his father's shop in Nuremberg around Christmastime, and now you know that he is not just a nutcracker, but also a prince. And now you know the tale of the hard nut, why people say 'that was a hard nut to crack!', and how the nutcracker became so ugly."

Thus the judge ended his story. Marie thought that Princess Pirlipat was a cruel, ungrateful brat, and Fritz said that if the Nutcracker was worth anything he'd quickly defeat the Mouse King and get restored to his former self again.

CHAPTER 10

Uncle and Nephew

If any of my dear readers have ever cut themselves on glass, then they know how badly it hurts and how dreadfully slowly it heals. Marie had to spend almost a whole week in bed because she became dizzy whenever she tried to get up. But at last she recovered and could run and play as merrily as before.

The glass cabinet had been repaired as good as new and was again filled with trees, flowers, houses, and beautiful dolls. Marie was thrilled to see her beloved Nutcracker standing on the second shelf smiling with all of his teeth intact.

As she looked at her favorite toy, she remembered the story Drosselmeier had told of the history of the Nutcracker and his quarrel with Lady Mouserinks and her son. She realized that her Nutcracker could be none other than the pleasant - but unfortunately cursed - young Drosselmeier from Nuremberg. The clockmaker from the court of Pirlipat's father could be none other than Judge Drosselmeier, which Marie had never once doubted. "But why... why didn't your uncle help you?"

It became clear to Marie that the battle she had seen was in fact a battle for the Nutcracker's kingdom and crown. Were not the dolls his subjects, and had he not fulfilled the astronomer's prediction by becoming their leader? As the clever Marie pondered over this, the more she thought of the Nutcracker and the dolls as living people, and she half-expected them to start moving about. But they remained stiff and motionless in the cabinet. But Marie, certain beyond any doubt that they really were alive, decided it was because of Lady Mouserinks's curse.

"But," she said to Nutcracker, "even if you can't move or speak, dear Mr. Drosselmeier, I know that you can understand me - I know it very well. You can count on me to help you, if you need it. At the very least I'll ask your uncle if he can help."

Nutcracker didn't move or stir, but Marie thought she heard a faint sigh and a gentle voice through the cabinet, just barely audible:

Little Marie,
Guardian sweet,
I'm yours to keep
Little Marie

A shiver ran down Marie's spine, but she was comforted nonetheless.

Dusk fell, and her father stepped into the room with Godfather Drosselmeier. Before long Louise had arranged the tea table and the family sat down and had a merry conversation. Marie quietly moved her little easy chair near Drosselmeier's feet and sat down. When everyone had quieted down she looked up at the judge with her big blue eyes and said, "Godfather Drosselmeier, I realize that the Nutcracker is your nephew, the young Drosselmeier from Nuremberg, and that he has become prince - no, king - as the astronomer had predicted, but you already know this - and that he is at battle with the son of Lady Mouserinks. Why don't you help him?" Marie once again told everyone about the battle and how it went. Everyone except for Fritz and Drosselmeier began laughing.

"Where does the girl get such ridiculous ideas into her head?" Dr. Stahlbaum asked.

"She's always had a vivid imagination," her mother said. "These are just dreams brought about by her fever."

"It's not true, any of it," Fritz said. "My hussars aren't such cowards. If they were, I'd personally discipline them."

But Godfather Drosselmeier put Marie on his lap and with an odd smile said very quietly, "Dear Marie, you were born a princess like Pirlipat, for you rule a bright and beautiful land. But you will have to suffer much if you are to look after Nutcracker, for the Mouse King will pursue him in every land and across any border. I cannot help him - only you can do that. Be faithful and strong."

Neither Marie nor anyone else knew what to say after that. The doctor took Drosselmeier's pulse and said, "You have, my esteemed friend, a severe head cold. I'll write you out a prescription."

But Mrs. Stahlbaum shook her head slowly and said quietly, "I think I know what he's saying, but I can't quite explain it."

CHAPTER 11

The Victory

It wasn't long after that incident that Marie was wakened one moonlit night by a strange rumbling that seemed to come from the corner of the room. It was as if small stones were being thrown about with squeaks and squeals mixed in.

"The mice - the mice have come back!" Marie cried in surprise. She wanted to wake her mother, but found herself unable to make a sound or move a muscle. She could only watch as the Mouse King squeezed himself out through a hole in the wall. His fourteen eyes and seven crowns glistened as he bounded through the room and made a huge leap up to the top of Marie's nightstand.

"Hee hee hee, I must have your sugar balls and marzipan, or I will bite your Nutcracker through!" he squeaked, and gnashed his teeth hideously. Then he jumped off the table and disappeared through the hole in the wall.

Marie was so frightened by his horrific appearance that the next morning she was very pale and could barely say a word. A hundred times she wanted to tell her mother, Louise, or at least Fritz what had happened, but she thought, "will they believe me, or will they laugh at me?"

But one thing was certain, and that was that she would have to give up her sugar balls and marzipan. She put each and every piece in front of the toy cabinet that night. The next morning her mother said, "I don't know how all these mice got into our living room - look, Marie! They've eaten all your candy!"

Indeed they had. The marzipan wasn't to the Mouse King's taste, but he nibbled it with his sharp teeth so that it had to be thrown out.

Marie wasn't concerned with the candy, however. She was quite happy inside for she believed that Nutcracker was safe.

But that night she heard a dreadful squeaking and squealing right by her ear. The Mouse King was there again and looked even more horrible than before. His eyes gleamed and he hissed more threateningly from between his gnashing teeth, "I must have more. Give me your sugar dolls, or I'll bite your Nutcracker through!"

And he jumped away again.

Marie was very sad. The next morning she went to the cabinet and looked mournfully at her sugar dolls. Her pain was not unreasonable - her sugar dolls were beautifully shaped and molded into figures even you might find difficult to believe. A shepherd and shepherdess looked after grazing flocks of milky-white lambs while their merry little dog scampered about, two mailmen walked with letters in their hand, and four handsome couples - men in dapper suits and women in beautiful dresses - rocked in a

Russian swing. Behind that there were dancers, then Pachter Feldkümmel and Joan of Arc, whom Marie didn't particularly care about. But in the corner stood a red-cheeked child, Marie's favorite. Tears welled from her eyes. "Oh!" she exclaimed, turning to the Nutcracker, "Dear Mr. Drosselmeier, I'll do everything I can to save you, but it's very hard!"

She looked at the Nutcracker, who looked so helpless that she couldn't help but imagine the Mouse King with all seven mouths open to devour the unfortunate young man. At that, she was ready to sacrifice everything. She took all of her sugar dolls and set them by the base of the cabinet as she had with the sugar balls and marzipan the night before. She kissed the shepherd, the shepherdess, the lambs, and her favorite, the red-cheeked child, which she put in the very back. Pachter Feldkümmel and Joan of Arc were put in front.

"Now that's too bad," Marie's mother said the next morning. "A very big and nasty mouse must live in the toy cabinet, because poor Marie's sugar dolls are all gnawed and chewed up."

Marie could not keep herself from crying, but she soon smiled again when she thought to herself, "what does it matter? Nutcracker is safe."

That evening, after Marie's mother told the judge about the damage caused by the mouse in the cabinet, Dr. Stahlbaum said, "it's a shame we can't exterminate that infernal mouse that's destroying Marie's candy."

"Hey," Fritz interrupted enthusiastically, "the baker downstairs has got a big gray cat I'd like to bring up. He'll take care of things and bite off that mouse's head, even if it's Lady Mouserinks or the Mouse King himself!"

Their mother laughed. "And jump around on tables and couches, knock down the glasses and cups, and cause a thousand other damages."

"Oh, no, he wouldn't," Fritz protested. "He's a clever cat. I wish I could walk as gracefully on the roof as he does."

"Please, no tomcats tonight," said Louise, who could not tolerate cats.

"Actually, Fritz has a point," Dr. Stahlbaum said. "But could we set up a trap? Or do we have none?"

"Godfather Drosselmeier can make one. He invented them," Fritz said.

Everyone laughed, and after Mrs. Stahlbaum informed everyone that there were no mousetraps in the house the judge announced that he had several, and within an hour he had gone to his home and brought back a splendid mousetrap.

The tale of the hard nut was very much alive inside Fritz and Marie's heads. When Marie saw Dora the cook (whom she knew quite well) browning the fat, all of the stories came rushing back to her head. She began to tremble and she blurted "oh my queen, beware of Mouserinks and her family!"

At that, Fritz drew his sword and said, "if any of them showed up here, I'd take them out!"

Later, as Fritz watched Drosselmeier bait the mousetrap and set it into the cabinet, he said, "careful, Godfather Drosselmeier, that the Mouse King doesn't play some trick on you."

That night, Marie felt something like ice-cold feet crawling up her arm and something rough and disgusting brush against her cheek. There was a horrible squealing in her ear - the Mouse King sat on her shoulder. He drooled blood-red, gnashed his teeth even more ferociously than before, and hissed into Marie's ear:

Don't go to the house
Don't go to the feast
Can't let yourself get caught
Like a wretched little beast
Give me all your picture books
Give me your Christmas dress
Or I'll nibble Nutcracker all to bits
And you'll never have any peace
Squeak!

Marie was miserable and visibly distressed. She was haggard and pale, and when her mother - who though that Marie was still upset over her candy and terrified of the mouse - noticed this she said, "I'm afraid that nasty mouse hasn't been caught yet." Then she added, "but we'll get it, don't worry. If the trap doesn't work, we'll have Fritz bring up the baker's cat."

As soon as Marie was alone in the living room, she stood in front of the glass cabinet and sobbing, said, "oh, Mr. Drosselmeier, what more can an unfortunate girl like me do for you? The Mouse King wants my picture books and the dress the Christ Child gave me - and when he's bitten through those he'll just demand more. I'm afraid when I run out of things to give him he'll want to bite me up instead. What am I supposed to do now?"

As Marie complained to the Nutcracker, she noticed a large spot of blood on his neck.

Since learning that the Nutcracker was really Drosselmeier's nephew, she no longer carried him about in her arm nor kissed him as she had before, and in fact she found herself becoming quite shy in front of him. However, she removed him from the toy cabinet and wiped away the blood with her handkerchief. Suddenly, she felt him growing warm in her hand - and even moving. She quickly set him back down, and he spoke with apparent difficulty, "my dear Miss Stahlbaum, to whom I owe everything, do not sacrifice your picture books or your Christmas dress for me. I just need a sword - if I had a sword, I could-"

And suddenly he stopped, and his melancholic eyes became still and lifeless once more.

Marie was no longer frightened or worried. In fact, she jumped with joy because she now knew how to save the Nutcracker without sacrificing any more of her treasured possessions. But where to find a sword? She decided to ask Fritz, and that evening after their parents had departed from the living room, told him the complete story of what had happened in front of the toy cabinet that fateful night, and what she had to do to save Nutcracker now.

Fritz had never thought over anything as hard than what he should do with his hussars after he heard from Marie how badly they'd performed in battle. He asked her very seriously whether it was really true, and after Marie assured him that it was he hurried to the glass-fronted cabinet and gave them a stern speech. Then he cut the insignias off their caps and forbade them from playing the Hussar's March for a year. Then he turned to Marie and said, "I can help Nutcracker with a sword. I just retired an old colonel of the cuirassiers with a pension yesterday, and he's got a bright and shiny sword he won't be needing anymore."

The aforementioned colonel was making use of his pension in the back corner of the third shelf. Fritz brought him out, removed his silver sword, and hung it from the Nutcracker's belt.

That night, Marie was so anxious she was unable to sleep. She could hear clattering and banging coming from the living room, and suddenly, "squeak!"

"The Mouse King - the Mouse King!" Marie cried, and jumped out of her bed in fright. For awhile it was completely quiet, then there was a knock at the door and a small voice said, "Excellent Mistress Stahlbaum, be of glad heart - for I have good news!"

Marie recognized the voice of young Mr. Drosselmeier. She threw on her dressing gown and opened quickly opened the door.

Nutcracker stood outside the door with a bloody sword in one hand and a candle in the other. He knelt down on one knee and said, "you, and you alone, my lady, have given me the courage of a knight to fight the insolent scoundrel who dared treat you so disrespectfully. The treacherous Mouse King now lies mortally wounded and wallowing in his own blood. Please accept, my lady, these tokens of my victory from your devoted knight." Nutcracker removed the seven crowns he had strung over his left arm and presented them to Marie, who accepted them gladly.

Nutcracker rose to his feet and said, "my excellent lady, with my enemy defeated I can now show you the most wonderful things, if you will kindly follow me for a short while. Please come with me - please come, excellent lady!"

CHAPTER 12

The Kingdom of the Dolls

I believe every one of you children would have instantly followed the honest and good-natured Nutcracker, who never had an evil thought in his head. Marie was glad to follow him all the more because of her gratitude to him, and because she was convinced he would keep his word. So she said, "I'll go with you, Mr. Drosselmeier, but it can't be too far or take too long because I haven't had enough sleep yet."

"Then we'll take the shortcut, though it is a bit harder."

He walked ahead and Marie followed him until they reached the big old wardrobe in the hall. To Marie's surprise, its doors - which were normally locked - hung open. She could see her father's fox-fur traveling coat hanging in the front.

Nutcracker nimbly climbed up the coat by grabbing onto its trimmings until he reached the large tassels that hung from its back. He pulled on one of them, and a little cedar ladder descended from the coat sleeve. "Please climb up, my dear lady."

Marie - who had somehow become as small as the Nutcracker in the meantime - did. When she drew close to where the collar ought to have been, she could see a blinding light through it. When she pulled herself up and her eyes adjusted, she could see that she was standing in a wonderfully fragrant meadow that sparkled like millions of shimmering gems.

"We are in Candy Meadow now," Nutcracker said. "But we'll soon pass through that gate."

Marie looked up and saw the beautiful gate, which was just ahead of them. It seemed to be made of white, brown, and rosy-colored speckled marble, but when she got closer she could see that it was really made of almonds and raisins baked in sugar. Nutcracker informed her that for this reason it was known as the Almond-and-Raisin Gate, though the common folk had rather disparagingly nicknamed it the "Student's Snack Gate."

A gallery made from barley sugar had been built out from the gate where six monkeys in little red jackets played Turkish marching music. Their music was so beautiful that Marie almost didn't notice that the marbled path that lead through the meadows was really made of beautifully-crafted nougat.

Soon they approached a grove with an opening on each end, and the loveliest smells drifted out from it. Although it was rather dark inside, gold and silver fruits hanging from the trees sparkled brightly. The branches and trunks were adorned with bouquets and ribbons like a joyous bride and groom and their wedding guests. When orange-scented zephyrs drifted through, the tinsel tinkled and clinked to make cheery music and twinkling little lights bounced about.

"Oh, it's so beautiful here," Marie said in delight.

"We are in Christmas Forest, excellent lady," Nutcracker said.

"I'd love to stay here awhile - it's so beautiful!"

Nutcracker clapped his little hands and immediately a few shepherds, shepherdesses, hunters, and huntresses appeared. They were all so white you'd have thought they were made of pure sugar. They had been about all along, but Marie had not noticed them while she'd been walking. They brought Marie an adorable little golden chair with a cushion of white licorice and invited her to sit down on it. No sooner than she had done so the shepherds and shepherdesses danced a magnificent ballet and the hunters blew their horns. When they finished, they all disappeared into the bushes again.

"Pardon me, excellent Lady Stahlbaum," Nutcracker said, "and forgive me that the dance turned out so badly, but the people are part of our wire ballet; they can't do anything differently; it's always and forever the same. And the hunters and their sleepy, dull blowing - that has its reasons, too. The candy hangs a bit high over their noses in the Christmas tree! Even so, why don't we move on?"

"I thought it was very pretty; I liked it quite well!" Marie said as she stood up and followed the Nutcracker.

Soon they came to a murmuring, whispering creek that seemed to be the source of the wonderful smells that filled the woods.

"This is Orange Creek," Nutcracker explained when she asked. "But aside from the lovely fragrance, it's not nearly as impressive as Lemonade River. They both pour into Almond Milk Lake."

Before long, Marie heard a louder rippling noise and saw the wide Lemonade River flowing in amber-colored waves between bushes as bright and green as emeralds and peridots. A cool, fresh scent that strengthened the heart and chest rose from the water. Not far away a dark yellow stream that smelled uncommonly sweet plodded along, and all kinds of pretty little children sat fishing at its banks. They pulled up small, round fish that they ate immediately. As she drew near, she noticed that the fish looked like hazelnuts.

In the distance a lovely little village sat near the river. The houses, church, parson's home, and barns were all dark brown, though the roofs were covered in gold. Many of the walls were painted with bright colors, as though they had been pasted with candied orange peels and almonds.

"That's Gingerbreadholm," Nutcracker said. "It's on the Honey River. The people there are nice to look at, but they're in terrible moods because they suffer from toothaches. So we'll pass them by."

Then Marie saw a small and beautiful town full of colorful and translucent houses. Nutcracker headed straight up to it.

Marie heard a ruckus and clamor and saw what had to be thousands of little people unloading carts that had been packed as full as they could in the marketplace. Upon closer inspection, their goods seemed to be multicolored paper and bars of chocolate.

"This is Bonbonville," the Nutcracker said. "Shipments from Paperland and from the Chocolate King have just arrived. The poor town has been threatened by the mosquito admiral, so they're covering their houses with donations from Paperland and building walls with the bars the Chocolate King sent them. But what we really want to see, excellent lady, are not these small country towns and cities. Let us hurry to the capital - the capital!"

Full of curiosity, Marie hurried after Nutcracker. Before long the air was filled with the scent of roses, and everything around them seemed to have a gentle rosy glow. She saw that the glow came from light reflecting from a body of rosy water that splashed with silvery-pink waves just ahead of them, and as they drew nearer she could see that it was really a large lake.

Silvery-white swans with golden collars swam about the lake singing the most beautiful songs in chorus while fish that shimmered like diamonds jumped up and down as if in dance.

"Oh!" Marie exclaimed. "That's the lake Godfather Drosselmeier promised to make me, and I'm the girl who will pet the swans!"

Nutcracker smiled a mocking smile she'd never seen before. "Uncle could never do anything like that; even you would be more likely to make a lake, dear Miss Stahlbum. But let's not worry about that right now, and sail across Rose Lake to the capital."

CHAPTER 13

The Capital

Nutcracker clapped his little hands again and the silvery-pink waves of Rose Lake came faster and higher. Marie could see what looked like a chariot made from a giant seashell covered with glittering gems in the distance. As it drew closer she could see that it was pulled by two golden dolphins. When it reached the shore, twelve little Moors with hats and tunics woven from glistening hummingbird feathers jumped off and took Marie, then Nutcracker onto the little sea-chariot and immediately took off again.

The golden dolphins raised their heads out of the water and blew crystalline sprays through their blowholes and sang in in silvery voices:

Who is this who crosses Rose Lake?
A fairy! A bumblebee!
Bim bim little fishes
Sim sim swans
Tweet tweet golden birds
Little fairy, come along
Come along the fragrant rosy waves

But the little Moors who were at the back of the sea-chariot didn't seem to like the dolphin's song very much at all. They shook their palm-leaf parasols so hard that the fronds they were made from rustled loudly. They stamped their feet in a strange rhythm and sang:

Click-a-clack
Clack-a-clop
The Moorish dance mustn't stop
Swim on, fishes, swim on swans
Roll along, shell-boat, roll along on
Click-a-clack
Clack-a-clop
Cloppa-clicka-clop!

"The Moors are amusing enough," Nutcracker said, sounding a little embarrassed, "but they're going to make the whole lake rebellious."

In fact, it wasn't long before a ruckus of voices from the air and the sea could be heard, but Marie wasn't paying attention. Instead, she was looking at the face of a lovely and charming girl in the rose-colored waters who was smiling up at her.

"Oh, look, Mr. Drosselmeier! Look down there! It's Princess Pirlipat and she's smiling at me! Please look, Mr. Drosselmeier!"

Nutcracker sighed sadly and said, "oh, excellent Lady Stahlbaum, that is not Princess Pirlipat, but your own face smiling up at you."

Marie sat up very quickly, closed her eyes, and felt very ashamed. At that same moment the Moors lifted her out of the sea-chariot and carried her to land. She was in a small thicket that was almost more beautiful than Christmas Forest. Everything shone and sparkled, and the fruits that hung from the trees were of the most unusual colors and smelled marvelous.

"We're in Marmalade Grove," Nutcracker said, "but there is the capital!"

And what Marie saw now! I will describe to you children the beauty and splendor of the city which opened into a wide meadow of flowers before Marie's eyes. The walls and towers were resplendent in beautiful colors, and their shape and design was like nothing else seen on Earth. Instead of roofs, the houses were topped with finely-wrought crowns and the towers were adorned with garlands of the most delicate multicolored foliage.

As they passed through the gate (which appeared to be made of macaroons and and candied fruits) silver soldiers saluted with with their rifles and a man in a brocade gown threw his arms around the Nutcracker's neck. "Welcome, excellent prince! Welcome to Confectionery City!"

Marie was not a little surprised when she saw young Drosselmeier recognized as a prince by the distinguished-looking man. Then she noticed the confused and noisy din of the city with its merry and joyous shouting, laughing, playing, and singing, and such was the noise that she was distracted from all other thoughts.

"Nutcracker, what's all this noise about?" she asked.

"Excellent Lady Stahlbaum, this isn't anything special. Confectionery City is a densely populated and merry city; it's always like this. Please come farther inside."

They had hardly taken but a few steps when they came to a huge marketplace. It was a glorious sight - all of the houses were made from sugar filigree, rows of pillars and arches were stacked high, and in the center of it all was an obelisk made of cake. On each side of the latter were four marvelous fountains that bubbled with lemonade, orangeade, and other delicious sweet drinks, and the basin was full of cream so thick you could have eaten it with a spoon.

But prettier than all of this were the people gathered together by the thousands. They laughed, joked, and sang - in short, they were the source of the noise Marie had noticed earlier. There were finely-dressed gentlemen and ladies of all sorts: Armenians, Greeks, Jews, Tyroleans, officers, soldiers, preachers, shepherds, clowns, and as many other kinds of people as there are in the world.

At one corner there was an even greater din and the people were scattering in all directions, for the Grand Mogul who had been carried in on a palanquin accompanied by ninety three grandees of the realm and seven hundred slaves had unexpectedly run into the annual parade conducted by the fishermen's guild, which comprised of five hundred members. Unfortuntely, a Turkish general suddenly had the idea to ride into the marketplace with three thousand Janissaries, and by an extra stroke of bad luck the Procession of the Interrupted Sacrifice came by singing and playing "Let Us Thank The Almighty Sun!" right up to the cake obelisk.

When all four of these parties met, there was a great pushing, shoving, and squeaking. There was suddenly a great wailing, as a fisherman had knocked a Brahmin's head off and the mogul had nearly been run over by a clown. The noise grew louder and it looked like a riot was going to break out when the man in the brocade robe climbed to the top of the cake obelisk, rang a bell three times, and cried out, "Candyman! Candyman! Candyman!"

Suddenly the din died down, and everyone was busy getting back to their business as best as they could. The processions involved got back on their tracks, the mogul was picked up and dusted off, and the Brahmin's head was put back on his shoulders. The merry din resumed itself and everything went back to normal.

"Who is this 'Candyman' they're talking about, Drosselmeier sir?" Marie asked.

"Excellent Lady Stahlbaum, the Candyman is an unknown but terrifying power which is believed to control the destiny of these people, and is the eventual doom of them all. They are so terrified of it that the mere mention of its name can quell the greatest turmoil, as the Lord Mayor has just demonstrated. When its name is mentioned no-one thinks any more of Earthly matters such as pokes in the ribs or knocks to the head, but stops and asks, 'what is the nature of man, and what is his fate?'"

Marie could not contain a cry of astonishment when she stood before a castle with a hundred towers shining with a rosy-red glow. Now and then rich bouquets of violets, narcissuses, tulips, and matthiolas were hung from the walls. Their dark and vivid colors contrasted against the pinkish-white plaster behind them.

The great expanse of the central dome and the pyramidal roofs of the towers were studded with thousands of twinking stars of gold and and silver.

"Now we're at Marzipan Castle," Nutcracker said.

Marie was completely lost in the sight of the magical castle, and it didn't escape her notice that one of the towers was completely missing its roof, which little men on scaffoldings of cinnamon sticks were working hard to build.

Before she could ask about it, Nutcracker said, "not too long ago this beautiful castle was threatened by devastation, if not utter ruin. The giant Sweettooth came along and bit off the roof of that tower and had even started in on the great dome, but the people offered him a whole district and part of Marmalade Grove instead, which he ate up and continued on his way."

At that moment a soft and pleasant music began to play and the gate opened. Twelve little pageboys walked out holding lighted clove sticks like torches. Each of their heads was a single pearl and their bodies were made of ruby and emerald. They were followed by four ladies almost as tall as Marie's Clarette, and their clothes were so beautiful and brilliantly-colored that she knew at once they were princesses. They tenderly embraced Nutcracker and shouted joyously, "my lord - my prince - my brother!"

Nutcracker seemed very moved by this display of affection and wiped tears from his eyes. He took Marie by the hand and said emotionally, "this is Lady Marie Stahlbaum, the daughter of a very respectable doctor, and the one who saved my life. Had she not thrown her shoe at the right time and later found me a sword, I would be in the grave, bitten to death by the Mouse King. Tell me, does Pirlipat, who was born a princess, compare to Marie's beauty, goodness, and virtue? No, I say! No!"

All of the ladies shouted "no!" and tearfully embraced Marie crying, "oh, noble savior of our brother, noble Lady Stahlbaum!"

The ladies escorted Nutcracker and Marie into the interior of the castle, into a room where the walls were made of pure sparkling crystals of every color. But Marie was most taken by the dear little chairs, tables, dressers, desks, and other furniture standing around made of cedar and Brazil wood and strewn with golden flowers. The princesses had Marie and Nutcracker sit down and immediately announced that they themselves would prepare them a meal.

The princesses fetched bowls and pots of the finest Japanese porcelain, as well as spoons, forks, knives, and graters and other kitchen utensils plated with gold and silver. The brought in the finest fruits and sweets, such as Marie had never seen before, and began to squeeze the fruits, crush the spices, and grate the sugared almonds with their delicate snow-white hands. They were so efficent in their work that Marie could see what expert chefs they all were and that she could expect a splendid meal. It was all so exciting to watch that she secretly wished she could help them.

As if reading her mind, the most beautiful of Nutcracker's sisters handed Marie a golden mortar and said, "sweet friend and rescuer of my brother, please crush this sugar candy."

Marie cheerfully crushed the candy in the mortar, which made a pleasant, almost musical sound. Nutcracker began to tell at length how he had fared badly against the Mouse King's army and how the cowardice of half the troops had lead to their defeat, how the Mouse King had wanted to bite him to pieces, how Marie had been forced to sacrifice many of his subjects in her service, and so on.

As Marie listened to him tell the tale, the sound of the mortar seemed to grow more distant and indistinct, and a silver mist seemed to rise out of the floor and surround the princesses, the Nutcracker, and evern herself. She heard strange singing, buzzing, and humming noises in the distance that seemed to draw closer, and felt herself rising as if on waves higher, higher, higher, and higher...

CHAPTER 14

Conclusion

Poof! Marie felt herself falling from an immense height. What a jolt!

Suddenly she opened her eyes and found herself laying in her little bed, and it was broad daylight. Her mother stood over her and said, "how can you sleep so long? Breakfast is ready!"

You have probably realized, honored listeners, that Marie, exhausted from her adventures, had fallen asleep at last in the hall of Marzipan Castle and the Moors, pages, or even the princesses themselves had carried her home and put her to bed. "Oh, Mama - Mama! Young Drosselmeier took me and showed me the most beautiful things last night!" Then Marie told her mother everything she saw, just as I have told you, and her mother looked at her in amazement.

"You've had a long, beautiful dream, dear Marie, but now you must put it from your mind."

But Marie insisted that it wasn't a dream and that it had really happened. So her mother took her to the glass-fronted cabinet and showed her the Nutcracker, sitting on the second shelf as usual. "How, silly girl, can you believe that a wooden doll can be alive and move?" she asked.

"But Mama, I know very well that Nutcracker is young Mr. Drosselmeier from Nuremberg, Godfather Drosselmeier's nephew."

Both of her parents broke out into peals of laughter.

"Oh!" Marie exclaimed, nearly in tears, "now you're laughing at my nutcracker, Papa! And he spoke so well of you! When we arrived at Marzipan Castle and he introduced me to the princesses - his sisters - he called you a respectable doctor!"

But they only laughed harder, and Louise and Fritz started to laugh too. Marie quickly went to her bedroom and retrieved the seven crowns of the Mouse King, which she presented to her mother. "Look, Mama, these are the crowns of the Mouse King, which Nutcracker gave me last night as a token of his victory."

Her mother marveled over the tiny crowns, which were made of an unknown but brilliant metal and seemed impossible for human hands to have forged. Even her father was completely fascinated by them, and they both asked in ernest where she had gotten them. She could only repeat what she had said before, and when her father scolded her harshly and even called her a little liar, she began to cry violently and said to herself, "oh, poor me, poor me - what am I to say?"

At that moment the door opened and the judge stepped through and shouted, "what's happening? Why is my godchild Marie crying? What's going on?"

The doctor informed him of all that had happened while he showed him the little crowns. However, the judge had hardly listened to a word of it when he laughed and said, "what a silly fuss! These are the crowns I wore for years on my watch chain. I gave them to Marie for her second birthday. Have you forgotten?"

Neither one of them could remember such a thing. When Marie saw that they were no longer angry, she ran up to Godfather Drosslemeier and said, "you know everything, Godfather Drosselmeier. Tell them that Nutcracker is your nephew, young Drosselmeier from Nuremberg!"

But Godfather Drosselmeier frowned and muttered, "ridiculous foolish nonsense."

Then the doctor took Marie aside and said very seriously, "listen, Marie, forget all these tall tales and foolishness. If you ever insist that the nutcracker is Drosselmeier's nephew again, I will throw not only the Nutcracker, but all of your dolls - Madam Clarette included - out the window."

Of course Marie could no longer speak of it, but her mind was filled with it nonetheless. You can well imagine that if you'd seen anything so marvelous yourself, you wouldn't be able to forget it, either.

Even Fritz would ignore Marie if she ever began to tell him of the fantastic realm that had delighted her so. It's even rumored he would occasionally muttered "silly goose!" between his teeth, but given his usual good demeanor I find this doubtful. This much is certain, however - he no longer believed what Marie had told him earlier and made a formal apology to his hussars with a public parade, replaced their lost field insignias with taller, fancier goose feathers, and allowed them to play the Hussar's March once more. However, you and I know just how pathetic those hussars were when those nasty little balls left stains on their red jackets!

Although Marie couldn't talk about her adventure, the images of that marvelous fairyland and its lovely sounds played over and over in her mind. Instead of playing with her toys, Marie would often sit still and silent as she remembered it all. The others would scold her and call her a 'little dreamer.'

It happened one day that as the judge was repairing one of the family clocks, Marie sat next to the glass-fronted cabinet remembering her adventures. She looked up at the Nutcracker and suddenly found herself saying, "dear Mr. Drosselmeier, if you really were alive, I wouldn't be like Princess Pirlipat and hate you because you stopped being handsome for my sake!"

At that moment the judge cried, "foolish nonsense!"

But there was suddenly a bang so loud that Marie fainted from her chair. When she awoke, her mother was looking over her. "How can a big girl like you fall off your chair?" she asked. "Anyway, the judge's nephew from Nuremberg has just arrived, so behave yourself."

Marie looked up. The judge had put on his spun-glass wig and yellow coat and was smiling happily. He held the hand of a small, yet handsome young man with a face as white as milk and red as blood. He wore a beautiful red coat trimmed with gold, shoes and stockings of white silk, a powdered wig, and a splendid braid down his back. In one hand he carried a most delightful bouquet of flowers and under his other arm he carried his hat, which was woven from silk. The small sword at his side was encrusted with flashing jewels.

The young man was polite and well-mannered. He gave Marie all sorts of toys and replaced the marzipan and sugar dolls the Mouse King had chewed up. To Fritz he gave a beautiful sabre.

At the table he cracked nuts for everyone; even the hardest could not resist him. With his right hand he put the nut in his mouth and with his left hand he gave a tug on his pigtail, and - crack! - the shell broke into pieces.

Marie had blushed a fiery red when she first saw the young man, and after dinner she blushed even redder when he invited her to come into the living room to the glass-fronted cabinet.

"Just behave when you play, children," the judge said. "Now that all the clocks are telling the right time I've nothing against it."

Hardly were they alone when young Drosselmeier knelt down on one knee and spoke thus: "my most excellent lady Stahlbaum, you see at your feet the happy Drosselemeier, whose life you saved right here. When you said that you would not hate me like the cruel Princess Pirlipat for whose sake I became ugly, I immediately ceased to be a hideous nutcracker and and received my former and not-unpleasant form again. Oh noble young lady, please make me happy by giving me your worthy hand and sharing my kingdom and crown. If you do, you shall reign with me in Marzipan Castle, for there I am king!"

Marie took him up by the hand and said, "dear Mr. Drosselmeier, you are a gentle and good man, and also since you rule a country with such wonderful people I accept you as my bridegroom."

With that, they were engaged. In a year (so they say) he came to take her to his kingdom in a golden carriage drawn by silver horses. When they were married in due time, there were twenty-two thousand of the most brilliant dancers dressed in pearls and diamonds to entertain at the wedding, and to this day Marie should still be the queen of a country in which shimmering Christmas forests and glazed marzipan castles - in short, the most marvelous things you can imagine - can be seen if you only look.

Printed in Poland
by Amazon Fulfillment
Poland Sp. z o.o., Wrocław